B is for Boston
Copyright © 2014 by Dry Climate Inc.

Printed in the United States

ISBN
978-0-9856429-6-9

Library of Congress Control Number
2014918207

B is for Boston

Written by Maria Kernahan

Illustrated by Michael Schafbuch

A is for aquarium, New England's underwater park.

Peek into the coral reef and get **this close** to a shark.

B is for Boston, the home of Paul Revere's ride. American history is a source of our pride.

C is for Cape Cod with miles of sandy shore.
Find a stretch of empty beach
and bring your Labrador!

D is for the ducklings that all year are on display.

But if they started waddling,
we surely would make way.

E is for the Esplanade which runs along the river.
On the Fourth of July the Boston Pops deliver.

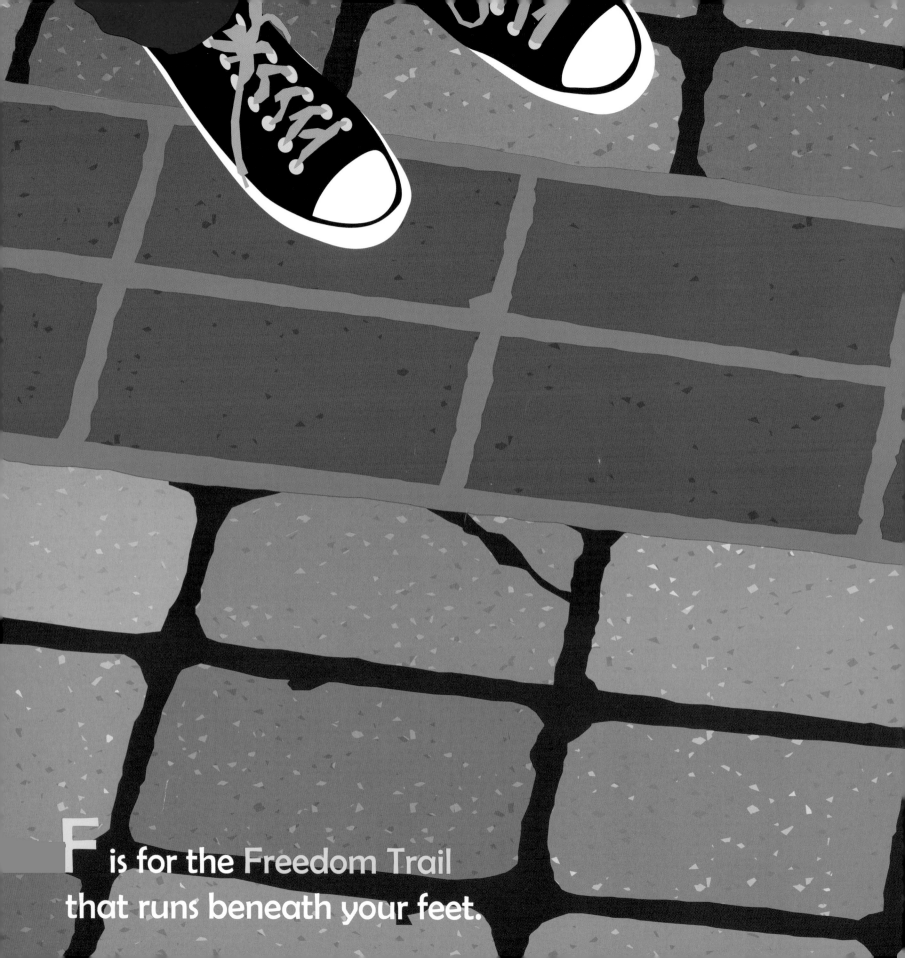

F is for the Freedom Trail that runs beneath your feet.

Follow the medallions
through Boston's cobbled streets.

G is for the Green Monster
standing guard at Fenway Park.

If you can hit a home run here,
you've really made your mark.

H is for the harbor that leads out to the sea. It's famous for the Patriots who dumped out all their tea.

I is for Harbor **Islands,**
a quick ferry ride away.

It's here that you can swim and hike
or kayak for the day.

J is for the jerseys worn by our favorite teams.

Every season we start fresh with championship dreams.

K is for the Kennedy Library
where history is on display.

It celebrates the president that we call JFK.

L is for lobster, the big red crustacean.

Prized and delicious, it's the best in the nation.

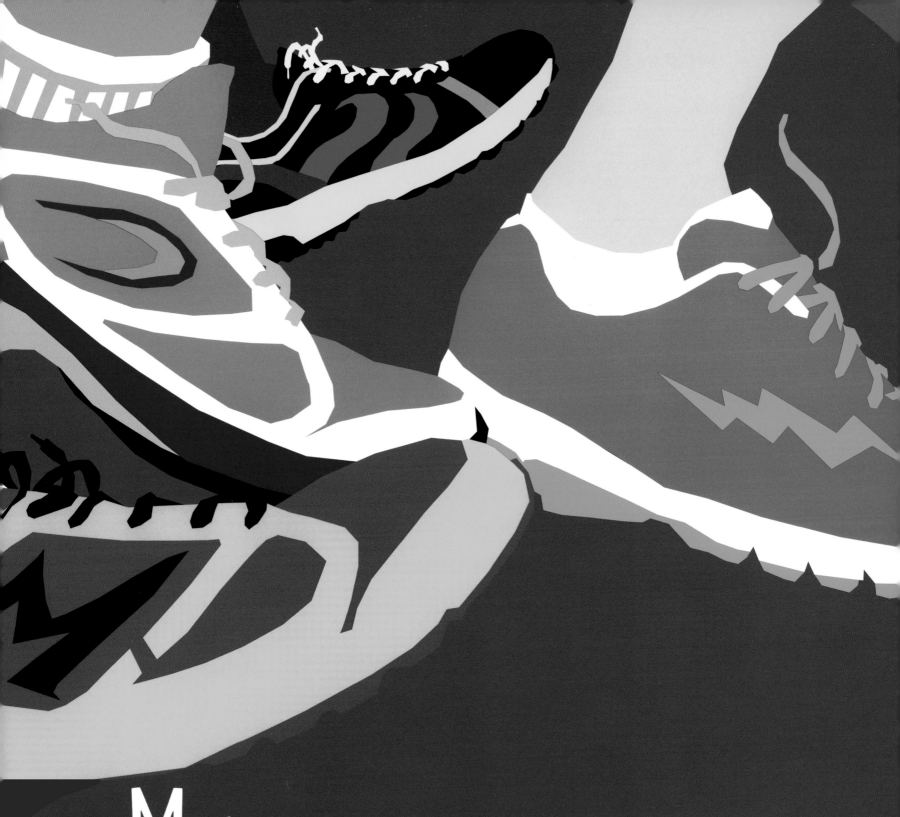

M is for the **Marathon**, a test of guts and will.
The hardest part of this long race
is climbing Heartbreak Hill.

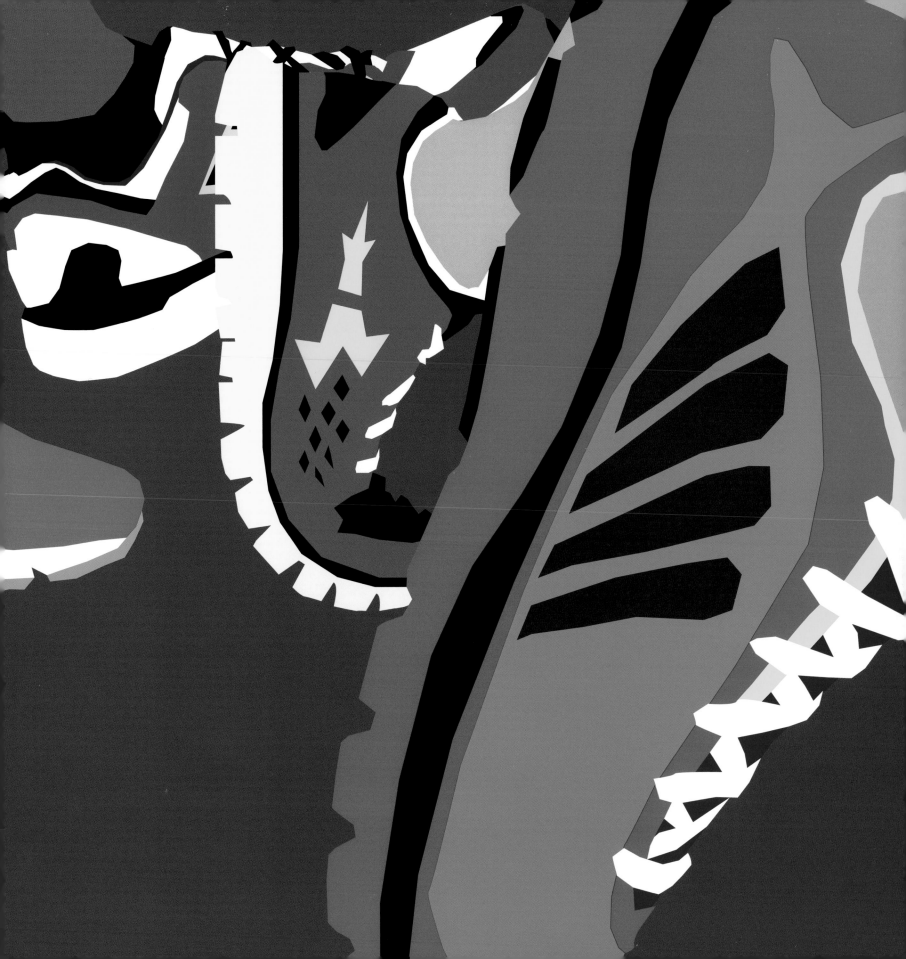

N is for the North End,
Boston's oldest neighborhood.

Sample some spaghetti here.
It's truly wicked good!

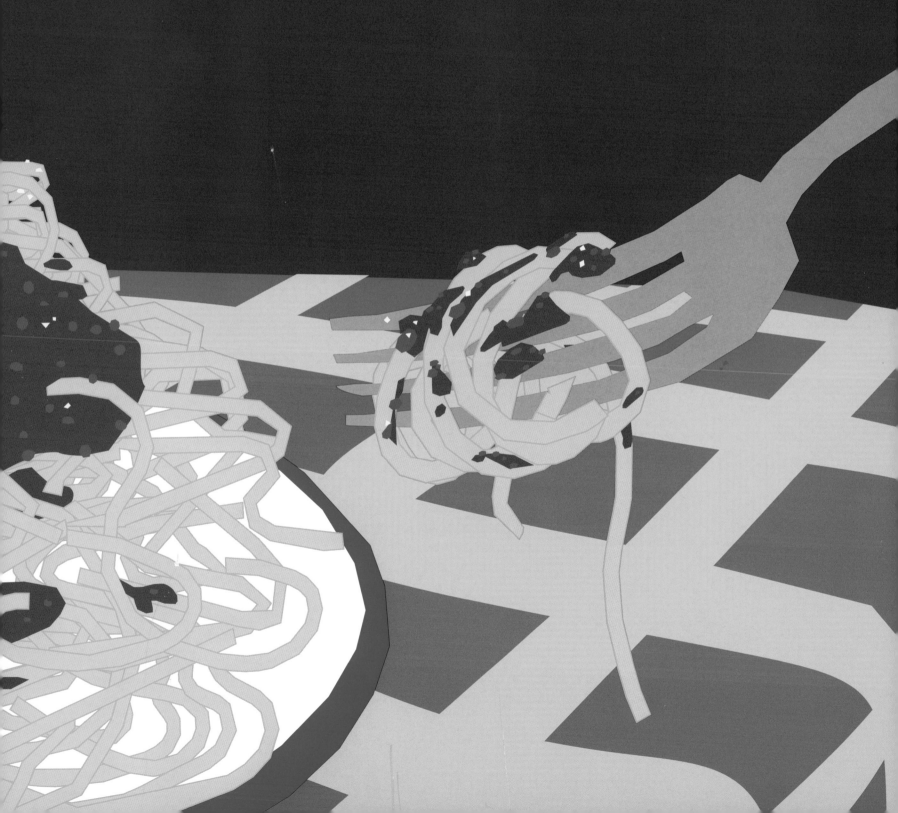

O is for Old Ironsides, the USS Constitution.

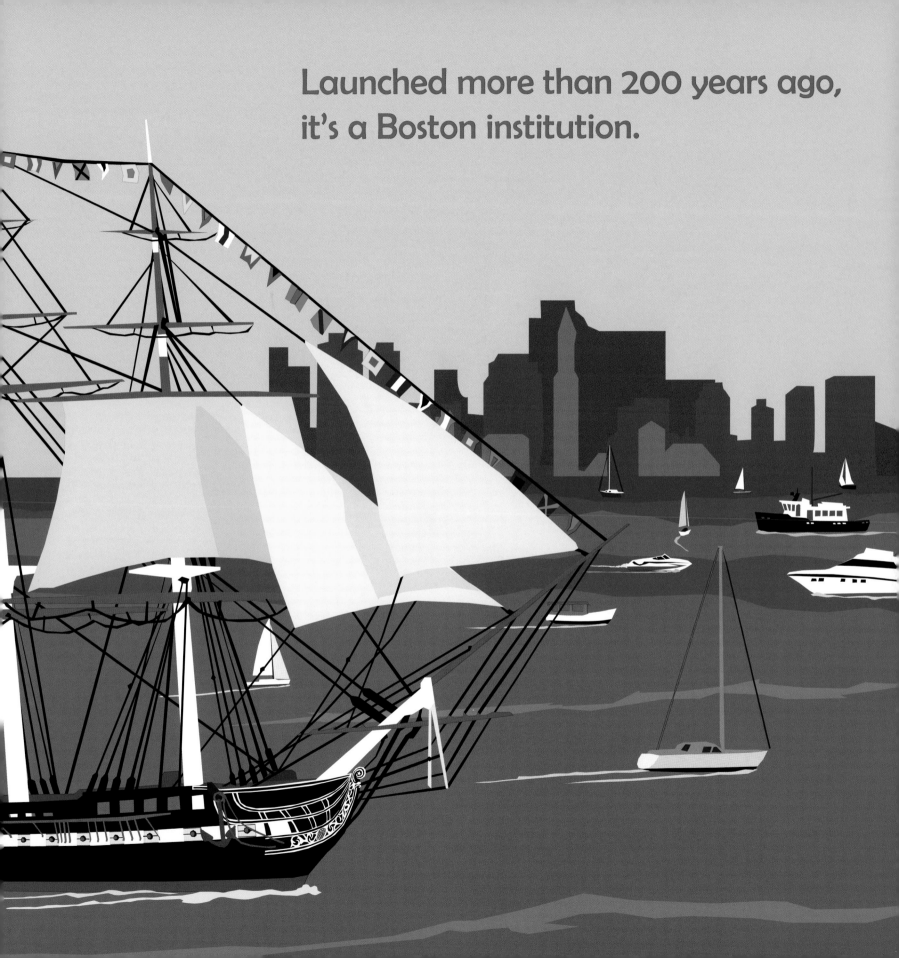

Launched more than 200 years ago, it's a Boston institution.

P is for the Patriots who fought against the King.

With muskets and with cannonballs
they let freedom ring!

Q is for Quincy Market across from Faneuil Hall.
A festival of food and art,
there's year-round fun for all.

R is for **rowing** in shells of eights and fours.

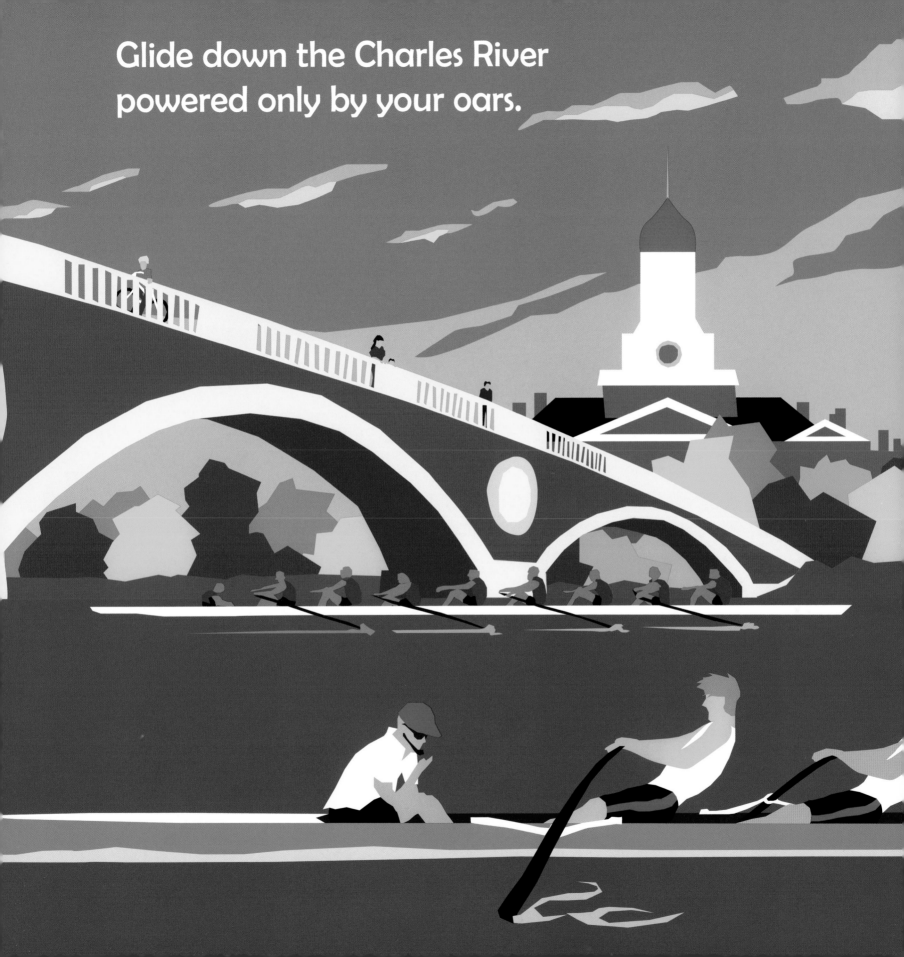

Glide down the Charles River powered only by your oars.

S is for the Swan Boats that float on the lagoon.
Take a ride around the park on a summer afternoon.

T is for the Ⓣ, Boston's way to get around.

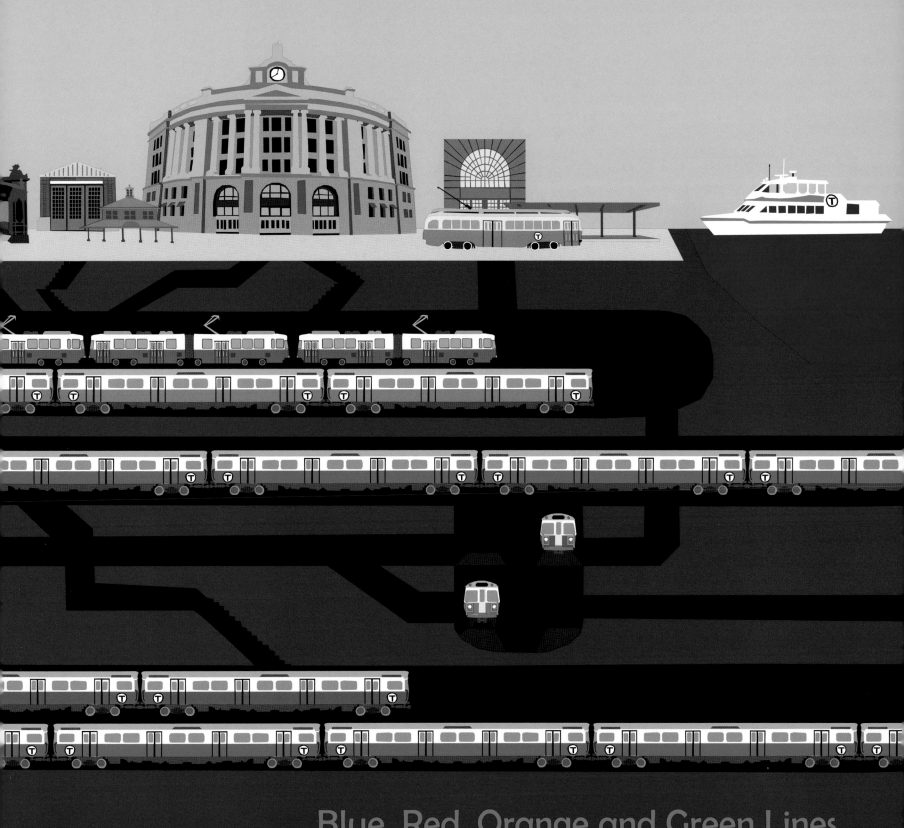

Blue, Red, Orange and Green Lines
will take you all through town.

U is for universities - Boston is a college town.

UMASS

MASSBAY

NORTHEASTERN

BABSON

HARVARD

QUINCY COLLEGE

BAY STATE

ENDICOTT

BRANDEIS

EMERSON

Berklee

SIMMONS

NEW ENGLAND LAW

MOUNT IDA COLLEGE

BENTLEY

PMC

BUNKER HILL

LC LASELL

Labouré College

NECB

BOSTON ARCHICTECTURAL COLLEGE

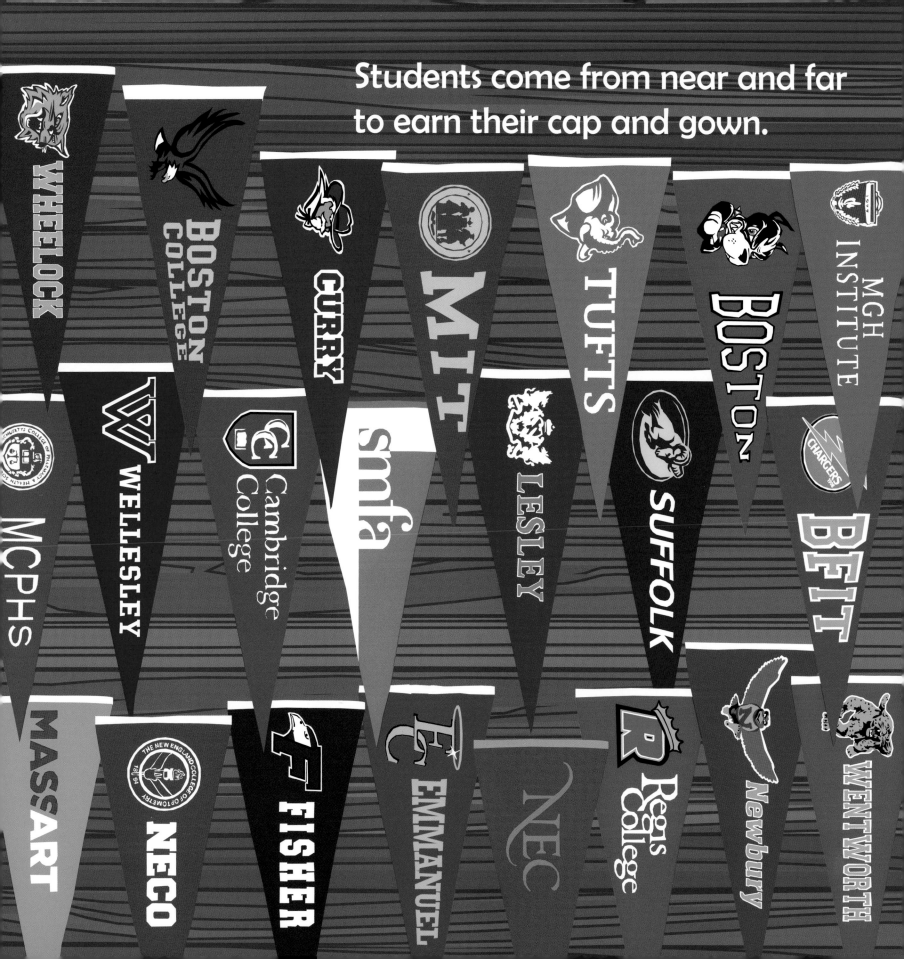

Students come from near and far
to earn their cap and gown.

V is for The Vineyard, an island off the Cape.
Getting there is half the fun, the trip's a great escape.

W is for whale, have you seen the great humpback?

The mother totes her baby
like a little whale backpack.

X is for the **X**s around the Frog Pond rink.

Bundle up against the cold
or your cheeks will get quite pink.

Y is for the yummy donuts

found on every street.

Frosted, glazed, or powdered,

they're Boston's favorite treat.

Z is for the **Zakim Bridge,**
so strong and sleek and fine.

It can carry lots of cars
or 14 elephants in a line!

Thank you

T is for Thank you, it's not just a letter.
Your help was amazing, it made us much better.

Christopher and Matthew, Meggie, Claire and Libby,
Maureen and Big Daddy.

Thanks to the families that helped by reading early drafts.
We need the extra eyes, big and little!

The Frothinghams
The Gales
The Hibbards
The Kourtzes
The Laughnas
The Levy-Howards
The Malins
The Parrishes